# *Learning Curve*

## By
## Melissa Kendall

Copyright © 2016 by Melissa Kendall
ISBN: 978-1-68361-031-1
Cover art by Tibbs Designs

Published by Decadent Publishing Company, LLC
Look for us online at:
www.decadentpublishing.com

## ~A Note from the Author~

Dear Reader,

Sometimes when you finish a book and write 'The End' that is where the story ends. But in the case of Sally and Dean from Curve My Appetite they felt they had more to say and so Learning Curve was born.

Madame Eve may have helped them find one another. But meshing their two worlds together isn't as easy.

As always I hope you enjoy this tale. If you want to share your thoughts send me an email at mkendallauthor@gmail.com

Be safe and enjoy!

### *Melissa Kendall*
www.melissakendall.net

# Chapter One

**D**ean's smile disappeared as he strode down the concourse toward the exit. His friend and manager, Jerry, waited for him with an angry scowl on his face.

Two weeks at the beach with Sally had been a revelation. Like coming out of some sort of weird emotional coma, he could see everything with crystal clear clarity. He hated that he hadn't even been back in LA a whole hour, and bitter resentment already replaced the giddy joy she'd instilled in him.

Jerry poked him in the chest. "You are not doing this."

Obviously, sending his manager an email to give him a heads up about his plans had been a bad idea. Standing tall and proud, unwilling to be intimidated, he replied, "I can do whatever I want. It's my life."

"Ha! That's what you think." Jerry's raised voice echoed more than it should have in the large space, catching the attention of passing passengers.

"We are not doing this here." He could see the headlines now—*Mark Martin and Manager have Screaming Match at LAX*. The last thing Dean needed was the paparazzi, who always hung around the airport, getting wind of a possible scandal.

"Fine," Jerry huffed. "But after what happened today, I'm not letting you off easy." He turned and stomped toward the exit.

*Damn him.* His friend always knew how to arouse Dean's curiosity. Moving fast, he followed Jerry outside. They walked side by side in silence the long distance to where the car was parked. Every minute it took, he itched to ask what Jerry meant, but he knew his manager well enough to know he wouldn't answer until he was god damn good and ready.

"Well?" Dean asked once they were safe and out of earshot inside Jerry's Mercedes Benz. "What happened today?"

"Hang on a sec. Let me get out of this zoo." His

friend started the car and navigated his way out of the parking lot. The entire time, Dean tapped his fingers on his knee, certain his manager made him wait on purpose. He wished the guy would just spit out whatever he thought was so important.

What seemed like hours later, they reached the freeway. "So?" Dean barked, impatience getting the better of him.

"So," Jerry responded. "Emmy nominations came out today."

*That's all he wanted to tell me?* "What's so special about that? I always get nominated." For the last five years, he'd received nominations for Outstanding Lead Actor in a Drama Series. Not once had he won.

As he mulled over the insignificance of the news, it occurred to him he'd gone to the Daytime Emmys before visiting Sally. He had to be talking about a different set of nominations.

He stared at Jerry. "Are you telling me I got nominated for a primetime Emmy?"

"Yep." His friend sounded so smug, a giant grin on his face. "Outstanding lead actor miniseries or movie."

*Holy crap.* "Jesus that's big. I' mean, I knew I'd been getting some good reviews for *Thieves and Liars,* but I didn't realize...." *Wow!* He turned to Jerry. "This is big, right?"

"Yes it's big. Frickin' huge, to be exact. Which is why quitting acting to go live as some nobody in Middle America is not in the cards."

*Damn it. Why does it never rain but pours?* For years, he'd been hoping to move out of television and into movies, but he'd never quite been able to make the jump. Getting nominated for *Thieves and Liars,* the miniseries he'd shot for HBO the previous year, would open a multitude of doors.

Didn't mean he would change his plans about quitting *Love My Family* or leaving LA to move to North Carolina with Sally. He loved her, and he'd waited his whole life to find a woman as perfect for him as her. No way was he giving her up for the sake of his career.

"Doesn't mean I changed my mind."

"What!" Jerry exclaimed, a what-the-fuck look on his face.

"I can't do *Love My Family* anymore." He sighed,

the exhaustion of almost a decade playing the same character evident in his tone. "And I am sick of living in LA. I'm too old for all the crap."

Jerry wrung his hands against the steering wheel. "Geez, that chick Madame Eve set you up with must have one golden pussy."

"I'd watch your mouth if I were you," he growled, clenching his hands into tight fists in his lap. "Sally is extremely important to me, and I hope she is going to be in my life for a very long time. If you want to remain my manager, then you better get used to it." In all the years he'd known Jerry, he'd never wanted to punch the crap out of him until right then.

"Jesus, you're serious," his manager replied, slack-jawed. "Do you love her?"

"Yeah." He sounded sappy even to his own ears. "I do."

\*\*\*

Dean walked in the front door to his condo and glanced around. Everything sat in its usual place, mail on the sideboard, house cleaned. Yet, he felt unwelcome. Six hours ago, Sally had dropped him off at the airport in Greenville. It had been hell to leave her standing there, eyes glistening with tears. He'd be lying if he didn't admit he might have had to wipe a tear or two from his own.

After setting his bag on the floor, he fished his cell out and unlocked it. He loved the speech-activated feature. "Sally." Immediately the phone dialed her number. Counting the rings—after five it would go to voicemail—he breathed a sigh of relief when she picked up on four. "Sally."

"You're home." She sounded happy but sad at the same time.

Hearing her voice eased the ache in his chest, at least a little. "Yep, baby, I'm home."

"Did you have a good flight?"

"Yeah, pretty good. I missed you, though. Wished you were with me." The sad sigh from the other end made him want to take the words back.

"Please don't say that. It's hard enough, me being stuck here with summer school and you being over two thousand miles away, with no idea when I'll see you again. Don't make it harder."

*I'm such a jerk.* "I'm sorry. I didn't mean to make you unhappy. Just wanted to let you know you were on my mind." He had known the moment he arrived on Sally's doorstep for his surprise visit he'd found the woman he wanted to be with for the rest of his life. The time they spent alone, the past fortnight, being together and learning everything about one another only served to heighten his feelings.

Sally sniffed. "I've been thinking of you, too."

Not wanting them both to end up in tears, he decided to change topics. "Hey, I got some good news when I arrived home today."

"Oh, really. What?"

"Guess who got nominated for a primetime Emmy?"

"Wow, that's terrific. What did you get nominated for?"

"Outstanding Lead Actor for *Thieves and Liars*."

"I loved that miniseries. You played a drug-addicted detective so well."

He stood a little straighter, chest puffed out. "Thank you." Dean had no idea what else to say. Sometimes he forgot she was a Mark Martin fan and had probably seen everything he'd ever done. "Anyway, I was wondering…. I know it will be right after school starts, but I hoped you might be able to get some time off to accompany me to the ceremony."

A weird squeak accompanied an "Oh, my God." Then silence.

He had to choke back a chuckle. "You still there?"

"Um, yeah. Sorry. Just a little shocked. You sure you want to take me?"

"Of course I want my girl there with me on what could be the biggest night of my career." Dean had hoped their time together, enjoying each other's bodies, might have rid Sally of some of her insecurities, but he could imagine the negative thoughts rolling around in her brain. "Please," he begged.

"Okay," she replied so quietly he almost didn't hear her.

"Okay? You're sure?"

"Yep," she said in a much more convincing tone.

"Woohoo! We're going to the Emmys."

# Chapter Two

Sally stared at the phone in her hand. *What the hell did I just agree to?*

The two weeks of sun, romance, and amazing sex seemed to have addled her brain. *I can't go to the Emmys.* An image of her college boyfriend bragging to his friends about how he conned the fat chick into giving up her virginity so he could pledge Phi Kappa, and them laughing like it was the funniest thing they'd ever heard, flitted into her mind and sent a shiver down her spine.

She texted Jodie. *911.*

The response came almost instantaneously. *Be there in 10.*

Unable to sit still, she paced back and forth in her living room. Her memory from college morphed into the Emmys' red carpet, and, instead of Josh and his friends laughing at her, in their place stood the world media.

*God, I'm such an idiot.* She'd meant to say no; the word had been on the tip of her tongue. Then he'd begged in that tone of voice he used on her in bed. Her affirmative answer had slipped from her lips before she'd even realized she'd said anything.

The eventual knock on her front door came as a welcome relief from her mental self-flagellation.

"I thought it would take you a couple of days before your meltdown after he left," Jodie said as Sally pulled the door open. Sally wanted to be angry at her best friend for making her sound so fragile, but she hadn't said anything that wasn't true.

She'd barely been holding it together, having Dean gone. All the way home from the airport, she'd fought back tears and reminded herself he would be back. Eventually.

She waved her best friend inside. "This isn't about him being gone."

"Well, what is it about?" Jodie moved into the living room and sat down on the couch.

Sally joined her, sitting on the other end, her legs tucked underneath her. "I'm going to tell you something, but you have to promise to keep it a secret. You can't tell anyone."

Her best friend nodded, a cautious smile on her face. Why had she asked Jodie to keep it a secret? Dean's nomination would be all over the news. Truth be told, she didn't think she could handle others' opinions right now.

"Dean has been nominated for an Emmy and has asked me to go with him to the ceremony. And I sort of said yes."

A scream echoed around the room, and her best friend jumped across the couch, wrapping her arms around Sally. "Wow! That is so exciting."

"No, it's not." She wriggled out of the embrace. "It's fricking terrifying."

Jodie stared wide-eyed at her like she'd lost her mind. "What on earth are you talking about?"

"I'm going to look like a joke standing next to Dean. He's Mark Martin, TV sex god, and well...." She waved her hand up and down her body. "I'm me, frumpy nobody."

"Oh, don't be ridiculous," Jodie scoffed. "Remember how amazing you looked in your dress for your one-night stand. I am sure we'll be able to find you something equally as amazing for the Emmys. Oh my Lord, it's so surreal to say. You're going to the Emmys."

Sally wanted to share in her best friend's excitement, but the feeling of dread creeping down her spine wouldn't ease.

"Okay, so the Emmys are in September, which means we've got about six weeks to get you the perfect outfit." Her friend prattled on about everything that needed to get done, but Sally tuned her out.

*Six weeks?*

A month and a half was enough time to lose a few pounds. It wouldn't hurt to use her gym membership instead of letting it gather dust in her purse.

"Thank God it's summer. I think we should head up to New York for a couple of days and get your dress there."

Jodie's words broke her out of her thoughts. "Huh?"

"Well, you're never going to find an appropriate dress here in Greenville, and New York is just a day's drive away. Figured we could make a bit of a road trip out of it."

Planning a road trip would provide her friend with the perfect distraction. "Okay," she replied. "But let's make it toward the end of August in case Dean changes his mind." And to give her at least a month to shed a few pounds.

After Jodie headed home, Sally dragged a trash bag into her kitchen. She emptied all the junk food from the fridge and the cupboards into it before changing into to her workout gear and heading for the gym.

Sitting in her car in the parking lot, she stared at the entrance. She'd been about to get out when two Barbie doll look-alikes in skintight spandex headed inside.

She wished she had a magic wand—one wave and she could make herself skinny. Real life, however, didn't work like that. The only way to lose weight was through hard work and dedication, not hiding in her car.

She sucked in a deep breath and then blew it out long and slow. "You can do this." She got out of her car and walked inside, her chin tucked to her chest. She was so busy trying to make herself invisible, she almost smacked into the door as a buff twenty-year-old exited.

"Sorry." She tripped over her feet and stumbled through the door, managing to catch herself before doing a face plant.

"You okay?" he asked.

"Yeah I'm fine." Her cheeks caught fire, and she wished she'd left when she had the chance.

"Can I help?" a young man behind the reception desk asked.

"Uh...." She looked over her shoulder to make sure he talked to her. "Just wanted to use the treadmill."

"Are you a member?"

She nodded and handed him her unused card.

He scanned it into a card reader then handed it back. "Have a nice day."

"You, too," she replied and headed for the machine room.

Opening the door, she sighed in relief, grateful to find it empty. She found a treadmill, hung her towel over the handrails, and hopped on.

She pressed the power button and had to hang on for dear life to stop from falling flat on her face. It had been while since she'd been to the gym, and it appeared they had newer, more electronic machines since the last time she'd been. The belt moved below her feet at a much faster pace than she'd anticipated. She pressed a button she thought would slow the treadmill, but it made it incline.

As her heart beat a rapid pace in her chest, she slammed her hand on the power button, bringing the demon machine to a stop.

"Do you need a hand?"

She looked up to see one of the women from earlier standing in front of her treadmill. Every fiber of her being wanted to say no. She could figure out a stupid treadmill all on her own. She suspected, however, the blonde glamazon had witnessed her almost face plant, and she didn't want to risk embarrassing herself any further.

"Yes, that would be great. It was set a little fast for

me."

Obviously familiar with the settings, the woman stepped around to the side of the treadmill, pushed a few buttons then pressed start. "There, it should be slower now." This time, the belt moved at a much more sedate pace. "So this button," the woman said, "controls the speed, and you press here for faster and here for slower."

"Thank you," Sally replied and smiled. She may have been jealous of the woman's size-four figure, but her mama taught her to be grateful when someone helped her.

"You're welcome, any time. I'm Candy, by the way." She held out her hand. "I teach an aerobics class here three nights a week. You should come by sometime."

"Sally." She shook Candy's hand. "Maybe I will." The idea of being surrounded by a room full of women who looked like Candy made her want to puke, but if she planned to go to the Emmys with Dean, she would need to get used to it.

The last thing she wanted to do was embarrass him in front of the world media.

# Chapter Three

"Cut! And that's a wrap for today."

*Oh thank God.* Dean had thought the torture would never end.

Not for the first time, he wished he hadn't signed to do this movie. It had seemed like a great idea a few months ago. Lead in a romantic comedy, one actually intended for release in theaters. However, after a half day lip locked with his co-star, wearing nothing but a cock sock, he just wanted it to be over.

He'd kissed his co-stars before, done sex scenes, too, so, he wasn't unfamiliar with the whole concept. Since meeting Sally, though, the feel of another woman's lips made his skin crawl.

*Why does it feel like I'm cheating?* If only he knew, then the lead weight on his chest would go away.

"Hey, Mark, can you come here a minute?" David, the director yelled his stage name.

As he sauntered behind the cameras, his heart thumped an erratic beat. In his experience, being summoned by the man in charge wasn't a good thing. "Hey, David, what's up?"

"I was going to ask you the same thing."

"Nothing's up. Why?"

"Well, then maybe you can tell me why it took us so long today to get this scene complete."

Dean stared at the director, unsure what to say.

"You were stiff as a board, today, and half the time you looked like you'd rather be anywhere but in bed with Lexie."

*That's because I would.* But the truth wouldn't fly. "Sorry. I had a hard time feeling it today."

"Well, you'd better get your head screwed on straight before tomorrow, or I'm going to start wondering whether you were the right choice for the part."

Without waiting for Dean to respond, David turned and walked away.

All the way home, the director's words echoed in his head. He'd thought he'd covered up how uncomfortable he felt better than he had.

Walking in the front door, Dean headed straight for the bar, a stiff drink in order after the day he'd endured. After pouring two fingers of scotch into a tumbler, he sat in his favorite recliner right as the phone rang.

Moving swiftly, he managed to grab the handset before the answering machine kicked in. "Hello"?"

"Hey, you," came the cheerful tinkle of his girl from the other end of the line.

Two little words and all the tension he'd been carrying on his shoulders slipped away. He sighed.

"'Hard day?" Sally asked.

Sitting down, he took a sip of scotch. "Yeah, today wasn't so great, but hearing your voice makes it all better."

Even from thousands of miles away, he heard her happy little hum and could picture how she looked. "Want to tell me about it?"

He took another sip. "Not sure you'll want to hear

about how awful filming a sex scene was today."

The moment the words were out of his mouth, he wanted to shove them back in. Nothing but silence echoed down the line. *Crap!*

"I'm sorry," he said. "It's just been a crappy day."

"No, no it's all right. You caught me off guard." The joyfulness had disappeared from her tone. "I knew you would have to be with other women as part of your job, but hearing about it brought it all home."

He couldn't stop the sad chuckle slipping from his lips. "You say it like I enjoyed it. Believe me, I didn't. Most of my day was spent nearly naked in bed with Lexie, and all I could think about was you. How awful having some other woman's skin touch mine was and how much better your lips felt. Every time I thought of you, my body would respond, and then I'd have to think of something awful to kill my semi. Then the director would yell at me for pulling a face. It was an awful, vicious circle, and I felt like I was cheating on you...." He didn't know what else to say, and the continued silence from the other end of the phone unnerved him.

"You hated it?" she finally asked, sounding

surprised.

"Of course I did. She wasn't you. It was like being in bed with a pile of bones and plastic." Sally's laugh made his heart skip a beat. "I kept wishing I was curled up naked with you. My hands on your luscious breasts, my cock buried in your hot, wet pussy." A sexy little moan echoed down the line, sending all his blood flow pounding towards his dick. "Like the sound of that, do you?"

"Gah, sorry. I just miss you. The mere thought makes my body respond."

"No need to be sorry, baby. One little whimper from you, and I'm hard as a rock." Solidifying his point, he ran a hand over the monster trying to escape his pants, groaning at the contact.

"Oh no, that's not fair, please don't. I don't want to be all wound up when there's nothing I can do about it."

Dean couldn't hold back his chuckle. "Oh, darling, who said there's nothing we can do about it?"

Sally gasped, following it up with a noise that sounded half moan half whine. "It's not the same without you."

"I'm not going anywhere. I'll be right here on the other end of the line, soaking up every sound you make. You know how much your noises turn me on." The way his cock twitched in his pants as she groaned in response only emphasized his point.

Undoing his pants, he sighed in relief at being free from constraint.

"What are you doing?" Sally asked.

"Undoing my pants. I think you should do the same. Why don't you take off whatever you're wearing?"

"I don't think I can do this. I've never done it before."

The apprehension in her whispered reply almost made him think twice about pushing the issue. His heightened state of arousal, however, overrode his rational mind. "Come on, darling. Think of me as your own live fantasy, there's nobody but you and me. You've got me so hard and horny. You want to help relieve the tension, don't you?"

Though she didn't say anything, there was a distinct rustling sound. *Please let her be getting naked.*

Taking the opportunity while she disrobed, he shoved his pants down to his knees and ripped off his shirt. A moan echoing down the line had him putting the phone back to his ear fast.

"What are you doing, beautiful? Tell me exactly what you're doing to your gorgeous body."

"I'm playing with my nipples. I miss you so much. Every time my thoughts drift to our time together, I get so wet." He listened hard, almost certain he could hear how wet. "But getting myself off just leaves me feeling empty. I need your cock in me. Nothing else will do. My fingers are no substitute...." She moaned a long low sound, one he had heard many times, and he stroked his cock faster.

"Oh, baby, my hand is no substitute for your pussy either. I miss the amazing wet heat of you wrapped around me, your walls contracting against my cock, squeezing out every ounce of pleasure."

"Oh yes! I want that so bad."

"Are you playing with your pussy, baby?"

"God, yes. Please don't stop talking. I want to hear what you'd do to me if you were here."

"Fuck, baby. I would bend you over so your

luscious ass was in the air. Then I'd fill you so full of my cock you could feel it everywhere."

"Yes, yes, yes!" The panting and moans coming from his love made it hard to concentrate. His balls tightened, his climax so close he had to ease off, not wanting to come until Sally did.

"Are you close?"

"Mmhmm…. What would you do to me once you had me full of your cock?"

"Oh, baby, I would fuck you so hard and fast. Pounding into your tight wet heat, making sure to hit the precise spot where you need me to."

"Oh God! I'm going to come."

"That's it, baby, let me hear how much you want me fucking you. How much pleasure it brings you."

The words were barely out of his mouth before Sally screamed, "Fuck, Dean."

Unable to hold back any longer, he let go, ecstasy washing over him, his body vibrating with pleasure.

After what felt like hours, his heart stopped pounding and his breathing returned to normal. "You still there?"

"Yeah," came the dreamy-sounding reply. "Thank

you."

"You're welcome, but I should be thanking you. I needed that after the day I've had."

"I needed it, too. It wasn't as good as having you here with me, but it was a hundred times better than doing it by myself."

An empty feeling hit him square in the chest. He longed for nothing more than to be able to wrap his arms around her and hold tight, soaking up her sated bliss. The memory of having done so many times before played on repeat in his mind. Cuddling and holding Sally had become one of his favorite things to do.

He had a weekend off coming up. He couldn't wait six weeks to see her. He'd surprise her with a visit.

After wishing her a good night and cleaning up, he sat in front of the computer and booked his tickets.

*Greenville, here I come.*

# Chapter Four

"D amn it." *What do I have to do?*

The numbers on the scales mocked Sally. Three weeks of exercising every day and eating tiny fat-free meals and she'd not even lost a pound.

Just yesterday, she'd argued with Jodie. Her best friend had noticed her lack of eating and constant exhaustion and taken it upon herself to stage an intervention of sorts.

"Sally, you're my best friend and you know I love you, but running yourself ragged and starving to death is not good for you."

"I'm fine," Sally barked, regretting the harshness of her tone.

"You're not fine. Look at you. It is not even seven

o'clock and you can't keep your eyes open for more than a few minutes. 'You're yawning nonstop. This is not a healthy way to live."

Sally snapped her mouth closed, trying to stifle the yawn that threatened. It didn't help—a loud yawn escaped anyway. "I'm fine, really. So I'm a bit tired. It's only temporary. As soon as this stupid ceremony is behind me, believe me, I will be back to normal."

"That's why you're doing this? God, I have half a mind to call Dean and tell him what you're doing to yourself."

A knock on her front door yanked her back to the present. A quick glance at the clock—ten to nine—had her wondering who would be visiting so late on a Friday night.

Opening the door, it took her a second to realize she wasn't hallucinating. Two steps and Dean's big strong arms wrapped around her. She'd missed his embrace so much. "What are you doing here?"

"I have the weekend off and I missed you, so I thought I'd come visit."

Sally sank into his warmth, grinning madly. "God, I missed you so much."

Her lips collided with his in a chaotic, passionate duel, each trying to devour as much of the other as possible. She thanked her lucky stars he had hold of her, otherwise, she'd have melted into a puddle on the floor.

When the need to breathe became overwhelming, she pulled back, gulping in what air she could. She stared into his gorgeous baby blues and let all her exhaustion fade away, replaced by intense arousal. Grabbing his hand, she dragged him inside, intent on getting him into her bed.

As the door slammed closed, Dean stopped, pulling her to a halt. "My God, what are you wearing?"

A quick glance down and her cheeks heated at the overabundance of skin visible through her threadbare T-shirt. "They're my pajamas. I was heading to bed."

"Well that sounds like an excellent idea." With a cocky grin on his face, Dean took over the dragging, moving in long strides toward her bedroom.

Once inside, he pulled her into his arms again, overwhelming her with a kiss. Every nerve in her body caught fire. "You're so fucking beautiful." He pulled away and started removing his clothes. "I need you naked, *now*."

All too happy to comply, Sally whipped her shirt off and slid her panties down to her ankles before stepping out of them. She stood, and her heart skipped a beat at the hungry animalistic expression on his face. He devoured her with his gaze, her body responding as if he had his hands on her.

"On the bed," he growled, removing the last of his clothing.

She wanted to obey, but she couldn't stop ogling him. In just a few weeks, her memories of naked Dean had faded. The reality before her was so much better than her fantasies.

"Keep looking at me like that and I won't be able to go slow."

Climbing onto the bed, she winked over her shoulder. "Who said I wanted you to go slow?"

In the blink of an eye, she went from kneeling on the end of the bed to lying on her back pinned to the mattress.

Nothing felt as good as the sensory overload swarming her every time her skin came in contact with Dean's. A shiver racked her body at the feel of his hardness pressing against her mound. A quick tilt of her hips and she'd have him right where she wanted him.

"Uh-uh. I want a taste of you before we get to the really good part."

Starting in the spot right behind her ear that always drove her nuts, he kissed a path over her collarbone, between her breasts, and all the way down to the first wisps of hair at the top of her mound.

"I can't wait," she cried, the pleasure too much to take. "I need you in me. Please, it's been too long."

He looked up at her, his eyebrow cocked. "You sure?" He nipped at her labia, emphasizing his point.

"Yes, I'm sure. You can eat me next time. Please, I need you to fill me."

He gave a slight nod then reached over to the top drawer of her bedside table. She'd never been one to keep protection on hand—not until Dean came into her life. She said a prayer of thanks to whatever higher power had gotten her to buy more condoms just in case.

With rapt attention, she watched him sheath himself. The masterful way he handled his cock screamed power and she wanted to feel it so badly.

Moving between her legs again, Dean lined himself up with her entrance. Before entering her, he locked gazes with her, the emotion swirling behind his stare almost too much to take. Without looking away, he thrust forward, filling her in one swift move.

"Oh God!" she cried out, the overfull sensation making her feel like she'd explode at any second.

"Fuck. I've missed you." The strained words were a mumble as his lips met hers in a searing kiss, the rest of his body remaining motionless.

Needing him to move, she rocked her hips, changing the angle just enough that he slipped out a fraction.

"Stop moving or I'm going to come."

She couldn't look away. He was so beautiful in his torment. His scrunched-up face showed how much effort it took not to move, yet there was a feral edge to it—one she wanted more of.

Sally didn't want to wait. "That's the point, isn't it? Please, I need you to move."

He ran a finger from the middle of her forehead and down the side of her face, tucking a strand of hair behind her ear. He then continued to a trail all the way down to where her heart thudded an erratic tempo in her chest. "I will, beautiful. Give me a second. I want this to be good for you, too. And it won't be if I finish in two seconds."

Resigned to the fact she couldn't force him to move, she relaxed and let him take whatever amount of time he needed. After weeks of being alone, she was just thankful to have him here with her.

She'd almost reached the limit of her patience when he finally moved and withdrew until only the tip remained inside her then he plunged back in again. This was what she needed, what she'd longed for.

"So good," she exclaimed, wrapping her ankles across his butt and giving him an extra little push. "Again...faster, please."

Picking a steady rhythm, he pulled out then thrust hard back in. All coherent thought disappeared, her mind swirling with the ecstasy being heaped upon her body. She clung to his biceps, anchoring herself.

Her hips moved in time with his, tilting upward in time for him to collide with her clit on each stroke.

"Fuck!" Her vocabulary was reduced to swear words and moans, as the pleasure bubbled up inside, filling her from head to toe.

"So close," he groaned in her ear before nibbling the spot at the base of her neck.

Stuck on the precipice, Sally moved a hand down between their hips, rubbing a couple of fingers over her throbbing clit.

"That's it, baby, touch yourself." Dean sat up a little, looking at her hand touching above where his dick continued to plunge into her. "So fucking sexy."

She nodded in agreement, the feel of his dick sliding past her fingertips exquisite.

She wanted to draw it out, stay in the state of ecstasy for as long as possible, but she could see the strain on his face. He held back for her, and she rewarded him with what he'd waited for. One pinch and her body combusted, a firestorm of ecstasy coursing through every single one of her cells. Tilting her head back and closing her eyes, she reveled in the pleasure. Dean's cries, when he reached climax, sounded muffled as if coming from a great distance.

The pleasure ebbed, and her exhaustion returned, the battle to keep her eyes open a losing one. His lips met hers in a slow, sensual, emotion-filled kiss before he moved off her, disappearing into the bathroom.

Drifting in and out of sleep, she wasn't sure how she got under the covers or when Dean returned. However, resting her head on his chest, his arm tightly wrapped around her, she succumbed to sleep, safe in the embrace of the man she loved.

# Chapter Five

Dean's fantasies had nothing on reality. Waking up with the woman of his dreams naked and draped over his body, getting to spend all morning in bed with her worshipping every inch of her beauty...well, there were no words.

The moment he stepped onto the plane, he'd been plagued with fear their two weeks together had been a one off and the spark wouldn't be there, but the instant her face lit up at the sight of him, he was certain everything would be fine.

He'd noticed how tired she looked when he arrived but thought nothing much of it given the late hour. In the bright sunlight, as they meandered to the local diner, the dark circles under her eyes and the pallor of her normally rosy cheeks hinted at something more than a lack of sleep.

His imagination conjured up a million different reasons for her change in demeanor from the last time he'd seen her in person. None of them, however, were good reasons.

Entering Sally's favorite diner, they grabbed a booth at the back. He would let her order food and eat some  before he got to the bottom of the conundrum.

"How can I help you?" the waitress asked.

From the many times they ate at the diner on his last visit, Dean responded. "I'll have a hamburger with the works. She'll have a double cheeseburger with salad and extra mayo and—"

"No, sorry," she interrupted. "Can I just have a chicken Caesar salad with dressing on the side?" He stared in disbelief. "Oh, and I'll have a bottle of water." In all the times they'd eaten here, she ordered the same thing. When she introduced him to the diner, she'd told him they made the best burger she'd ever tasted and she never ordered anything else off the menu.

The waitress turned her attention back to him. "Drink for you, sir?"

"A Coke, thanks." He waited until the waitress was out of ear shot. "So, you going to tell me what's going on, or do I have to guess?"

Fear flickered a brief moment in her eyes before she managed to school her features into an innocent smile. "I have no idea what you're talking about."

He might have believed her if she'd been able to look him in the eye as she spoke. "So, guessing it is. Are you sick?"

"No, what makes you think that?"

"Well, let's see. You ordered a salad and water instead of your favorite burger and a thick chocolate shake. You have bags under your eyes that make you look like you haven't slept in weeks, and you walked here like you were being dragged to the gallows. What else am I supposed to think?"

She fidgeted with the napkin in her lap. "I'm just trying to eat a little healthier, that's all."

"Okay, if you won't tell me what is going on"—he reached into his pocket and grabbed his phone—"I'll call Jodie. I'm sure she'll be more forthcoming."

"No!" Sally screeched, tearing the phone from his hands. She huffed then her shoulders sagged. "Fine...I'm trying to lose weight."

One little sentence and the penny dropped. *God I'm such an idiot.*

He put his hand under her chin and lifted until she looked him in the eye. "Is this because of the Emmys?" She nodded, and he wanted the ground to open up and swallow him. "Baby, you don't need to lose weight."

"That's good because, apparently, no matter how little I eat or how much I exercise, I can't seem to lose weight. Two damn weeks living off bird food and exercising like a maniac and I haven't lost a single pound." Her hunched posture and dejected expression damn near broke his heart.

He stood and slid into her side of the booth, wrapping his arm around her shoulder and pulling her in close. "Ever thought maybe the reason you haven't lost any weight is because you don't need to? Your body is already at its optimal weight."

She scowled and cocked and eyebrow. "Are you telling me I'm supposed to be fat?"

"You are not *fat*. Curvy, yes. And they are the sexiest curves. Makes it hard for me to keep my hands to myself." To prove his point, he used the arm around her shoulder to go in for a subtle caress of her breast, putting his other hand on her knee and moving it higher than appropriate in public.

"Don't." She squirmed, pushing his hands away. "You're just saying so because you like me."

He winced and wanted to scream from the rooftops that "like" didn't even come close to how he felt about her, but it wasn't the right time.

"You're right. I do like you a lot, which should lend some weight to my words. You are perfect. Every guy in here is jealous of me sitting here with the most beautiful woman in the room."

"Pfft. Like that is true. If I'm so beautiful, I wouldn't have spent most of my adult life single and lonely."

"I like to think it was fate making sure you and I met. That and those other guys were idiots."

His heart beat double time when she smiled. "Yeah, they were a little."

"You have to know I don't want, need, or expect

you to lose weight. You are gorgeous just the way you are, and I am proud to have you by my side."

Sally blinked, unable to stop staring. What right did one man have to be so perfect? Good looks, great personality, everything a girl ever dreamed of in her Prince Charming.

"Thank you. I'd like to say I'm never going to worry about my weight again, but I know that would be a lie. It's still nice to hear you like me the way I am."

She leaned in and nibbled on his lower lip, and when he gasped, she took full advantage, sliding her tongue inside his mouth. Forgetting where they were, she clasped her hands around his neck and pulled him close, wanting to feel his hardness pressed against her.

"Stop!" Dean pulled free from her grasp. The joy she'd been feeling moments earlier faded at his rejection.

"Now don't look so sad," Dean said, angling her face so they were eye to eye. "I want nothing more than to push you down on the bench and have my wicked way with you. Unfortunately, it would mean giving everybody in this place a show. And, in this day and age when everybody's phones are video cameras, I reckon it would take all of a couple of minutes for that video to be up on the Web."

Embarrassed at her idiocy, she buried her head in her hands. "I'm sorry."

"Don't be sorry, sweetheart. I promise as soon as we finish our food I'm taking you home and we are going to pick up exactly where we left off."

Fortunately, their waitress showed up right then, placing their plates on the table. "Is there anything else I can get you?"

"Just the check," Dean replied, not even looking at the waitress but giving Sally a sly wink.

The mere thought of what he had planned had her pussy throbbing with need. Never before had the mere suggestions of sex had her so aroused. Since she met Dean, however, arousal was an almost constant state, especially when he looked at her like *she* was his next meal not the burger on the plate in front of him.

Eager to leave, she devoured her salad, thankful

she hadn't ordered her usual burger because it always left her a little sleepy afterward. Dean also wolfed down his burger, with all the finesse of a starving man seeing food for the first time.

With the food eaten and the check paid, he stood and offered his hand. "Come on. Let's get home. I have a promise to keep."

Sally placed her hand in his, more than happy to follow anywhere he led.

\*\*\*

Here they were again, at the airport, saying goodbye. Every time seemed to get harder. How many times could Sally say farewell to Dean before she got down on her knees and begged him never to leave her? She'd see him in a few weeks, but, still, the knowledge didn't make her feel any less sad and alone.

"Now don't look at me like that." He cupped her cheek. "It's only a couple of weeks until the Emmys. I'll be finished filming by then, and I plan on taking a well-earned break in North Carolina."

She smiled, looking forward to having him around for more than a few days at a time.

A shriek from off to her right had her turning to see what had caused the noise. "Oh my God! You're Mark Martin," a girl in her late teens yelled, jumping up and down like she had ants in her pants.

Dean shot an apologetic look Sally's way. His fame took some getting used to, but often she forgot altogether. Dean, her boyfriend, wasn't anything like her previous fan-girl-self had expected Mark Martin, daytime TV god, to be.

Stepping away, Sally faded into the background as he obliged the fan with a photo and an autograph. When the fan was finished and on her way, he grabbed Sally's hand and dragged her to a more secluded area of the terminal.

"I'm so sorry." He'd explained the first time some random stranger had accosted him that fans were all part and parcel of being famous. In fact, he'd apologized every time it happened. She leaned in and kissed him, hoping to ease his fears.

"It's fine. I know it is part of your job."

"Yeah, but it doesn't make me feel any better

about it." He kissed her with one of his panty-melting lip locks. She didn't think any man's kisses would ever compare to Dean's in their ability to set her alight without even trying.

"I'm going to miss you," she whispered.

"I'm going to miss you, too, but we will be together again before you know it. And, hey, you're off to New York this week, so I'm sure you'll be so busy you won't even have time to think about me."

Sally choked back a laugh. If he knew just how many times a day she thought about him, he'd wonder how she got anything done. His reminder about her road trip with Jodie made her want to groan. She didn't look forward to trying to find a dress for the Emmys. She hated shopping for regular clothes at the best of times; looking for a ball gown would be a whole other level of pain.

"Speaking of New York, I have something for you." Dean reached into his pocket and pulled out a business card, placing it in her hand.

"What's this?"

"It's the name and phone number of the stylist I use in New York. I have spoken to her already, and she is expecting your call. She'll help you find a dress, hopefully with a minimum of fuss. Give you more time to have fun while you're in the city instead of traipsing all over, visiting store after store."

Though skeptical, she threw her arms around him and whispered thanks in his ear.

"You're welcome."

The scowl on his face when he glanced at his watch told her their time was up. "I have to go, babe."

She kissed him one last time, promising herself she wouldn't cry. She would see him again in just a few weeks. This was a "see you later" not good-bye.

# Chapter Six

E ven in the morning hours, the bright lights of Times Square seemed to overpower everything, including the sun. Jodie had scored a room at a hotel within walking distance of the offices of the stylist Dean had recommended. The location allowed for a little sightseeing as they made their way down 7th Avenue.

Everything, and yet nothing at all, had changed since her last visit. Maybe the warm weather made it seem different because her previous trips had been in the winter. Still, there was so much to see.

"You're awfully quiet." Jodie bumped her shoulder against Sally's, breaking her out of her thoughts.

"Yeah, sorry. I guess I'm just nervous. I don't enjoy shopping." The thought made her skin crawl, hours upon hours of trying on different clothes and then having to look at herself in the mirror. *Torture.*

"This isn't normal shopping, though. You have your own stylist working to find you the perfect dress."

She appreciated Jodie's efforts to try to cheer her up, but the impending sense of doom wouldn't go away.

They walked the remaining couple of blocks in silence. They found the address, a refurbished industrial looking warehouse. Pressing the intercom, they announced themselves, and the door buzzed open letting them in.

The first thing Sally noticed in the main lobby was the distinct lack of an elevator. Stairs were her nemesis and always left her gasping for breath. She'd make a great first impression, wheezing like a pack-a-day smoker, by the time she climbed the six flights to the third floor.

"It's not going to kill you," Jodie joked, well aware of Sally's aversion to stairs.

"It might," she replied as she started climbing.

She stepped onto the landing of the third floor,

and her breaths came easier than expected. *Guess all the workouts helped some after all.*

The stairs led strait into a giant open-plan studio. Floor-to-ceiling windows on two sides flooded the area with light. Racks and racks of clothing, everything from haute couture to casual, covered the other two walls.

A petite brunette stepped out from behind one of the racks and headed their way. "Well, look at you. You're beautiful. Oh, I definitely have a dress for you."

Sally's heart swelled with joy right up until the woman walked up to Jodie instead of her. Typical. Nobody assumed the fat chick was the one dating the TV star.

"Oh, no," Jodie corrected. "I'm not Sally." She pointed in Sally's direction. "She is."

The expression on the stylist turned from a giant smile to frown. "Oh. Sorry for the mix-up. I'm Anastasia, pleased to meet you."

She walked to Sally, her hand out. She didn't want to shake the hand of the woman who'd insulted her, but she wouldn't stoop to being rude. She shook the stylist's manicured hand, taking the opportunity to give her a once over from up close. Her dark roots indicated her platinum-blonde hair wasn't natural, and being so near revealed her makeup was so caked on, it changed her facial features. *How does she judge me? At least what people see is the real me and not some fake overly primped princess.*

Anastasia spoke, interrupting Sally's internal bitching. "So, Dean told me you were going to the Emmys with him and need a gown?"

The "I can't believe he is taking you" tone Anastasia used made her want to blow a raspberry in her face. She took the high road instead. "Yep, that's correct."

"Well, I have hundreds of suitable gowns in here. What size are you?"

A cold chill crept up Sally's spine at the idea of telling the woman her dress size. A quick, reassuring glance at Jodie gave her the strength to continue. "I'm an eighteen, but if the sizing is large, I can sometimes fit into a sixteen."

Anastasia stared at her.

"Is that going to be a problem?" Sally asked when,

minutes later, Anastasia had still said nothing.

"Um.... Not exactly. I just don't having anything in your size on my racks."

Sally schooled her features. She didn't want this rude fashionista to see how much the words hurt.

"That's fine," Jodie jumped in. "We'll take our business elsewhere. I'm positive there's at least one store in this city who would love to have one of their gowns on the red carpet at the Emmys." She grabbed Sally's hand and dragged her toward the exit.

"Hang on a sec. I didn't say I couldn't help."

"Well, what are you saying?" Sally bit back.

"Can you give me an hour to get some samples couriered in?"

She wasn't inclined to say yes to the woman who had treated her so abominably, but she also didn't want to have to traipse all over the city looking for a dress. "Okay, one hour, but if you're not ready, then I am taking my business elsewhere."

Sally couldn't believe what she saw in the mirror. The reflection looked nothing like her normal dowdy self. Anastasia had surprised her and come through with an array of dresses. The stunning red strapless gown she had on made her look like she'd just walked out of the pages of a magazine.

"Wow," Jodie said from behind her

Sally had to agree with her exclamation. "Yeah, definitely wow." She turned to the left and right, checking all the angles to make sure she didn't look like some hippo from the back but even the rear view seemed perfect. "I think this is the one."

"*Wunderbar*," Anastasia said in her stupid faux accent.

"How much is it?" Sally asked.

"Oh, no, dear, this isn't the kind of dress you get to buy. You will wear it on loan as advertisement for the designer."

"Oh, okay." Sally wanted to crawl back into the hole she'd come from. She wasn't cut out for this. "So, what happens now?"

"We will pin up these alterations to the length and the bodice, take the address of where you'll be staying in Los Angeles, and the dress will be delivered to you, along with a hair and makeup crew, to get you ready for the evening."

"You are so lucky," Jodie said from behind her. "I would kill to be in your place."

Sally chuckled. "No need to go to those extremes. I'll gladly trade places."

"You will not. You are going to go, you're going to look stunning, you're going to be with the hottest guy there, and, most of all, you are going to enjoy yourself. How many times have we watched the Emmys and wished those people walking the red carpet were us? You're getting the chance to live out a dream. Don't let other people ruin it for you."

"Yeah, but that's the problem. This all feels like some fantastic dream, and I'm going to wake up and discover it was a joke played by my subconscious."

Jodie pinched her arm, and she squealed. "Ow, that hurt."

"It was supposed to hurt. You aren't dreaming, but if you don't pull your head out of your ass, it may become one."

Sally loved Jodie, but, right now, she could get fucked. Her fears weren't unjustified or imagined. Hollywood had very exacting standards when it came to women and how they should look. The last thing she wanted was to be made fun of on national TV where all her students, friends, and family could see.

\*\*\*

"So, what shall we do now?" Jodie asked.

Sally had no idea. They'd planned for the dress hunting to take the first day. "What do you want to do?"

"Well, we could do some common people shopping, or maybe walk up and down Fifth Avenue, staring longingly in the store windows."

"Or," Sally interrupted, "we could go see if I can find a pair of shoes and some lingerie I can afford to go with the dress I just picked out."

"Ooo, what an excellent idea." Jodie walked to the curb, stuck her hand out, and let out a shrill whistle at the passing cab. It was in the far lane, and Sally expected it to drive by. Instead, it cut in front of another car and pulled to a stop right into front of Jodie.

Jodie smiled at her. "Don't you love New York? Your chariot awaits."

Sally returned her friend's smile then climbed into the back of the cab.

"Saks Fifth Avenue, please," Jodie instructed the driver, and they were whisked off down the street.

"Why are we going there?" Sally asked. "Everything will cost a fortune."

"Because you're going to the Emmys. Stuff from Target won't cut it."

"Yeah, but I don't have enough money to be shopping at Saks."

"Yes, you do."

"What do you mean 'yes, you do'? I can assure you I do not have enough money in the bank or credit on my card to buy anything at Saks."

"Well...Dean may have FedEx'd me a credit card and told me to make sure you got everything you wanted no matter the cost."

Sally wasn't sure whether she wanted to laugh or cry. Dean didn't mean any offense, she had no doubt, but that didn't mean she'd spend all his money.

"Don't be mad at him," Jodie said. "The dude has got it bad for you, and he wants you to be the prettiest girl on the red carpet."

"Oh, I'm not mad, Jodie. But, I guess if I'm spending his money, I should get some very sexy lingerie as a reward."

Jodie let out a loud guffaw. "That's my girl. Let's go shopping."

# Chapter Seven

Sally stared at her reflection, and even she could admit she looked pretty damn good. It was amazing what plenty of money and a team of experts could do to a person's appearance. She wouldn't be winning any best dressed awards, but it would all be worth it when she didn't embarrass Dean.

At knock at the door startled her out of her musings. Dean had disappeared a few hours ago when the stylist arrived. She opened the door and thanked her lucky stars she held onto something because she might have passed out. *Damn He's fine.* She'd seen him on TV in a tux before and thought he looked fine, but the in-person effect was swoon worthy. She glanced up and met his gaze, surprised to see an almost feral stare.

"You are fucking gorgeous," he said, his voice gruff like he hadn't used it in years. He grabbed her hand and spun her around like a ballerina. "Man, I am going to be the envy of every guy there tonight." He pulled her into a hug and leaned forward as if he planned to kiss her, but she managed to stop him.

"What do you think you're doing?"

"Trying to kiss my beautiful girlfriend."

"Oh, no, you don't. You'll ruin my makeup, and we don't have time for it to be done again."

"Oh, yeah. I better not ruin my makeup either."

"Wait up a second. You're wearing makeup?"

"Yeah, of course. We're going to be on camera. It's almost mandatory."

Sally couldn't stop the guffaw bursting out of her mouth. Never in a million years would she have expected to be talking makeup with her boyfriend.

"What are you laughing at?"

"Nothing. It's just, talking makeup with you is kind of surreal. Come to think of it, you probably wear makeup more often than I do."

"Almost every day, baby." He pulled her in,

hugged her, and placed a peck on her forehead. "Come on, let's get going, or we're going to be late."

\*\*\*

Sally squeezed Dean's hand as their limo finally pulled up to where they had to get out. They'd been sitting in the long line of limos for an hour, inching forward at a snail's pace, but the moment had arrived. The noise from outside had her wishing she didn't have to get out, but this was his night, and she would support him.

"Here we go," Dean said as the door opened.

The noise increased tenfold. If it had been loud before, now it was deafening. She moved to put her hands over her ears but then remembered the world media would see her, so she had to grin and bear it.

From every direction, people screamed, "Mark!"

Dean smiled, waved at his fans, and helped her out of the limo. The moment her feet touched the ground, flashes bombarded her and made it hard to see. She squeezed his hand hard, silently begging him not to let go.

He pulled her into an embrace. "I've got you, now smile." He placed a kiss on her cheek then turned and faced the throng of paparazzi.

An usher came forward and moved them to the first red carpet interview, this one for live TV. Sally wanted to bolt when she saw Ben Appleton, the host of *Hollywood TV*, standing right in front of them. "And here is Mark Martin from *Love My Family*."

Mark stepped forward while she, thankfully, remained off camera. They talked about his nomination and what Dean wore, and then he was back, holding her hand, and they were being ushered to the next stop. This one a photo op. She tried to stand back out of the way, but he would have none of it, hooking his arm around her waist and holding her close. They smiled and tried to look in the right direction as the cameras clicked.

The usher returned and moved them farther down the carpet, where it was basically wash, rinse, and repeat. An interview followed by a photo op then another on-camera appearance. It took almost an hour to get from one end of the red carpet to the other, a journey that in practicality should have taken five minutes at the most. At last, they made it inside the theater away from the paparazzi and fans.

Sally put her arms around Dean's waist and hugged tight.

"You all right?" he asked.

"Yeah, just a little overwhelmed. It was kind of cool, though."

He chuckled. "It is, a little, but it can get a bit trying after you've done it for the umpteenth time. I'm sure it is the same with most jobs. They all have their good points and bad."

"Yeah, I guess you're right."

"Come on, let's go and grab a drink then I see a couple of people I need to say hello to."

***

With the ceremony close to starting, Sally and Dean had been escorted to their seats. She couldn't believe they were only three rows from the stage. She pinched herself to confirm she wasn't dreaming. Every direction she looked there were movie and TV stars. It felt odd to see a face, recognize the person, even know their name, but they were, in fact, a total stranger.

An announcement came on, advising two minutes to broadcast, and people raced to be seated, most of them seat fillers.

The house lights dimmed, the stage lights lit up, and then Bill Compton the comedian hit the stage. Watching the ceremony on TV could never prepare her for the spectacle of being right there in the theater. If she had to describe it, she'd say the Emmys were a cross between a Broadway show, a comedy gig, and a high school commencement ceremony. Amazing, yet boring at the same time. Little bits of action grouped into fifteen minute slots followed by five minutes of people frantically trying to get out of their seats before the commercial break finished.

The entire time, she sat next to Dean, holding his hand, leaning against his shoulder, and taking it all in. Every so often, he would provide a ridiculous fact he swore was true about a star.

About an hour and a half into the ceremony, the host came on after a commercial break and welcomed to the stage the two stars who would be announcing the nominees for Dean's category.

Sally listened as the stars bantered back and forth then read the names on the envelope. Dean's grip on her hand tightened, and she rubbed her other palm over the back of his, trying to ease his grip. When his name was announced as a nominee, he leaned in and gave her a quick peck on the cheek.

"And the winner is...." Sally held his hand as tightly as he did hers while the envelope was opened. "Mark Martin! For *Thieves and Liars*."

Sally jumped to her feet, clapping. *Oh, my God, he won!* Everyone else in the crowd stood as well, but Dean stayed in his seat.

She leaned over and whispered in his ear, "Are you okay?"

He nodded and stood, pulling her into his arms and squeezing her tight. Then he made his way to the stage. Every couple of steps, he stopped to shake a hand or receive a pat on the back. Then he was there, standing at the podium with the gold statue in his hand.

"Oh wow," he said in to the microphone. "This is unbelievable. I never thought it possible I would win.

There are probably thousands of people I need to thank right now, but I can't think of a single name. To all my friends and family, thank you for supporting me over the years. I would have never made it this far without you. Jerry, my manager, I know you're here somewhere. Guess you're gonna be busy. And, last but by no means least, Sally. This award would mean nothing without you in my life. Thank you."

She wiped a tear from the corner of her eye. She couldn't believe, after having been together less than six months, Dean mentioned her in his thank you speech.

The stage lights dimmed, and the audience lights came on. An usher appeared at the end of their row. "Ms. Austens? If you'd like to come with me?"

Sally followed the young man, unsure where they were going but hoping it was to Dean.

# Chapter Eight

Dean stared at the shiny, surprisingly heavy, Emmy in his hand. He still couldn't believe he'd won. He'd thought the prospect so improbable he hadn't even prepared a speech.

A knock on the door caught his attention. "Come in."

The door opened  a crack and then Sally peeked around the corner. She flung the door wide and ran at him. "Oh my God, you won!" He pulled her into a hug with one arm while trying not to drop his award. "I am so proud of you."

She stared at him, aglow with her happiness, and everything was perfect. The woman of his dreams in one arm and an award for those at the pinnacle of his craft in the other. He couldn't give up acting, he loved it too much, and he couldn't give up Sally for the exact same reason.

"Can I hold it?" she asked, staring at his Emmy.

"Yeah, but be careful with it. I might never get another one." He passed her his award and made sure she had a good grip on it before he let go.

She held it up and then turned her head from left to right like she looked at her reflection. "Wow, it's so beautiful and heavier than I thought. Thing has got to weigh at least five pounds."

"Six pounds twelve and half ounces to be exact."

She chuckled. "How on earth do you know that?" She handed the award back to him.

"Just some useless fact I picked up. In my twenties, I managed to score a job working backstage. I wanted to be the one receiving the award, and, what do you know, my dream came true."

"Yeah, dream big or go home." She hugged him tight and gave him a quick peck on the lips. "So, what do we do now?"

"Well, I have to go and do a little bit of press then we go back out to our seats for the remainder of the awards. After the ceremony, I'll need to put in and appearance at the Governors Ball, but once we are done there, I'm taking you back to my place, stripping you naked, and fucking you against the nearest flat surface."

She shivered, and his cock got rock hard. *Oh, yeah, definitely fucking as soon as possible.*

\*\*\*

Sally held tight to Dean's hand as they entered the Governors Ball. Strobe lighting of various colors flashed across the ceiling. It was a lot darker than she'd expected and the atmosphere a lot like a high class disco.

"Come on, let's find our table."

They wove through tables and chairs, having to stop every few steps to say hello to someone and allow them to congratulate Dean on his win.

Most of them ignored her, but a few did ask about her. Dean introduced her as his girlfriend every time, and she had to admit it felt nice.

They finally located their table, though no one sat

at it. Everyone seemed to be mingling. One glance in any direction and a who's who of stars sat around chatting like they were normal everyday people.

She leaned in and whispered in his ear. "This is so surreal. There are famous people everywhere I turn."

He smiled and then kissed her. "Come on, let me introduce you to a few of them. Me being famous and all. I see the director of my movie over there."

Said director was a man in his mid to late forties with gray hair and a small spare tire around his waist. "Hey, Dean, congrats on the win, man."

"Thanks, Brad. Let me introduce you to my girlfriend, Sally Austens." She held out her hand and almost pulled it right back when, instead of shaking it, he kissed the back of her hand. "Sally, this is Brad Golfink, the director of the movie I am shooting at the moment."

"Nice to meet you," she said, trying to wipe her hand on her dress without anyone noticing.

"Likewise." He looked her up and down, and the leer he gave her made her skin crawl.

A waiter, carrying a tray of champagne glasses, walked by. She grabbed not one but two glasses, downing the first one in a single long gulp.

"You okay?" Dean asked.

"Yeah, just needed to relax a little."

For about an hour, she followed Dean around the ballroom, remaining silent when no one spoke to her and being polite when they did. Everything went relatively well until Dean had to go to the men's room.

She sat at their table, eating a few of the canapés to help absorb the alcohol she'd consumed, when a shadow appeared over her plate. She looked up to see a very tall, very skinny blonde woman. "Can I help you?"

"I see you're the flavor of the month."

"I beg your pardon."

The chick put her hands on her hips and scowled. "He'll get rid of you like he does every girl he dates. He's not one to settle down. You may think you're special, but you're not."

Before she could respond, Dean came back to the table. "Crystal," he said, a look of disgust on his face. "What are you doing here?"

"I came with Marcus."

"Fine. Well, why don't you go back to your date?" The angry tension between the two of them was palpable.

Crystal harrumphed then walked away.

Dean sat in the chair next to Sally. "Are you all right?"

"Yeah. Who was she?"

"Crystal Beauregarde. We dated for a couple of months a few years back. Until I came home one night to find her screwing some other guy in my bed."

Crystal's attitude and words of warning made perfect sense now. The Barbie look-alike was jealous. "How awful."

"Not really. I'd been planning to break it off with her anyway. Come on. What do you say we go home?"

"You don't have to stay?"

"No. I've put in a few hours. We stayed for the food. No one's going to notice if we disappear."

"Well, in that case, lead the way."

***

Dean shut his front door as Sally removed her

shoes. Her ass looked delectable covered in red silk, perfect and round and.... Damn, he needed her.

"I don't know how you do it," she said, standing on the carpet in her bare feet, flexing her toes. "My feet are killing me, and I feel like I could sleep for a week."

He walked up behind her and wrapped his arms around her waist, pulling her tight against him. She sank into him with a sigh. Nothing compared to having her in his arms.

"I hope you're not too tired. Because I kind of planned on stripping you naked, bending you over the couch, and fucking you senseless." She rubbed her backside over his crotch and moaned. Oh yeah, he'd fuck her silly.

Sally stepped out his arms, moved a few paces away, then turned to face him. She reached behind her, and the snick of what had to be her zipper being opened held him frozen and dying to see what would happened next.

Sally stared at him, a cheeky grin on her face, then lifted her arms. Her dress fell to the floor, a pile of red silk at her feet. She stood there, wearing nothing but a pair of sheer black, very skimpy panties.

"Holy fuck!"

"So you plan on standing there staring all night." She hooked a thumb in either side of her panties and slid them off. *Gorgeous.*

Dean had never gotten out of his clothes so quickly. A few buttons may have been casualties of his haste, and he suspected he'd have to search for his cufflinks. He didn't care, though, as long as he was naked so he could feel her skin touching his.

Two strides and he had her in his arms, her soft skin so smooth.. He smashed his lips against hers, and she opened her mouth, granting his tongue access. Giving her a taste of what he planned to do with his cock, he plundered her mouth with his tongue. She wrapped her arms around his neck and pulled him closer like she wanted him to devour her— and he would, and not only her mouth.

He put his hands under her ass and picked her up enough so her feet no longer touched the floor then carried her the few paces to the couch, where he set her on the arm.

He moved his kisses from her mouth, slowly

making his way down her body, stopping at her collarbone, her breasts, and her stomach, until the Promised Land lay right there in front of his face between her spread legs.

He leaned in and traced a figure eight with his tongue from her entrance to her clit and back again. Sally bucked her hips and cursed up a storm. He put his hand on her hip to hold her still and did it again and again.

"Oh fuck!" Her cries of ecstasy spurred him on. He slid first one and then a second finger into her soaked vagina, and a curl of his finger had her shaking and screaming his name.

*Wow!*

Sally could barely believe each time with Dean just got better—which was ridiculous because, from the beginning, the sex had been fantastic. She looked up at him standing between her thighs, palming his cock, and her arousal flared to life again.

"I need you." She hooked her finger at him in a come hither motion, but he didn't move.

"How do you need me, sweetheart?"

How did she not need him? She could make a list with a millions ways and still keep writing. "In me. I need your cock in me. Please!"

"Your wish is my command."

He smirked at her, lined his cock up with her vagina, and slid home in one swift move. The pleasure mixing with the slight pain of his dick stretching her was exquisite and everything she'd ever hoped for—except— "What's the hold up? Why aren't you moving?"

"Sorry. You feel so good. I need a minute, or I'm going to blow my load."

Sally didn't want to wait a minute, but she would because it would be worth it. She wrapped her arm around his neck and pulled him close until their mouths were less than an inch apart. "Well, while we're waiting, why don't you kiss me with that delicious mouth of yours?"

He did as asked, and his hips started to move in time with his tongue. She wrapped her legs around his waist and held on tight as his thrusts grew harder and faster and wilder.

She broke away from his kiss, needing to breathe, and, as she did, she caught sight of his cock slamming into vagina. She stared, mesmerized.

"You like that, sweetheart, the way my cock gives you pleasure?"

"Oh, yes...very much."

He reached between them and rubbed her clit. "I need you to come, baby. I can't hold on much longer."

"So close ...." She rolled her hips, changing the angle, and on the next thrust, her climax washed over her, sending wave after wave of pure bliss coursing through her body.

"Oh fuck, Sally!" Dean's cry of pleasure as he stilled inside her was music to her ears.

All strength ebbed from her body, the sated post-orgasmic feeling settling in. Her grip on him loosened, and she fell back toward the couch.

"Whoa, I've got you." He wrapped his arms tight around her waist. "You all right?"

"Yeah, I just really need some sleep now."

"Come on, then. Sweetheart, let's go to bed." He pulled out and stepped back, his expression changing from contented to horrified.

"What's wrong?"

He stared at her pussy and his cock.

"Dean!" She poked him in the chest. "What's wrong?"

"I'm so sorry."

She'd missed something, but she but couldn't quite figure out what. "What on earth are you sorry for?"

"I didn't use a condom."

Sally stared at his dick for a second, and then she laughed, a full-on until-you-snort kind of laugh.

Dean scowled at her. "I don't understand what's so funny."

"I'm on the pill."

"You are?"

"I am."

He tilted his head to the side like he tried to put a puzzle together but couldn't get the pieces to fit. "But why? I thought you hadn't had sex for a long time before we got together."

"I hadn't, but I had really bad, painful periods, and my doctor put me on the pill to help regulate them."

He let out a long slow breath. "Oh, well then, in

that case, I can't wait to screw you bareback again because that was fan-fucking-tastic."

Dean scooped her up, despite her protests, carried her into the bedroom, and tucked her into bed before disappearing into the bathroom.

She didn't remember much after that other than the heat of his body cuddled around hers.

# Chapter Nine

Sally yawned, the shackles of sleep ebbing away. She snuggled into the warm rock she slept on, only to sit bolt upright. She looked down at the naked male chest in front of her, and the memories of the previous night came back to her. Oh, and what a wonderful set of memories they were. She'd never felt as cherished as she did while wrapped in Dean's arms.

His eyes fluttered open, and he smiled at her. "Good morning, beautiful. What are you doing all the way over there?"

"I might have woken up not sure where I was and freaked." She stared at her hands in her lap, her cheeks flushing. She could be so stupid sometimes.

"Why don't you come snuggle with me, then? I

liked having you in my arms."

She lay back down on his chest, but before she could get comfortable, the shrill ring of a phone echoed around the room.

"Crap. That's my manager's tone. He never calls this early unless it's important. I have to get it." He rolled over and picked up his cell off the table. "Hello?"

Sally could only hear one end of the conversation, but his scowl and the not so pleasant words meant it had to be bad news.

When he hung up the phone, an apologetic expression filled his face. "I'm sorry. Jerry has lined me up a bunch of post-win interviews this morning He's going to be here in forty-five to pick me up."

"That's all right. It's your job. I understand." Disappointment filled her, but she kept it hidden. Dean already seemed mad enough for the both of them.

"It's not all right," he growled. "You're going home today, and I'd hoped to spend this morning like we did last night. What time do you have to be at the airport anyway?"

"One thirty." She looked at the clock over her shoulder. "It's six thirty now, so we have plenty of time."

"Okay, well, I'm going to go and get ready for these interviews, but I'll be back by eleven and take you to lunch before dropping you off at the airport."

It was on the tip of her tongue to ask if she could tag along to the interviews so she could spend more time with him, but he hadn't suggested it and she didn't want to make a nuisance of herself, so, instead, she said, "Okay."

Dean headed into the bathroom, and Sally huddled in bed.

She waited until he'd left before she got up and went through her morning routine. Once she'd dressed and packed her overnight bag, she headed into the kitchen. The coffee sat in the machine, warm and waiting. *Thank you, Dean for taking the time to put it on before you left.* She then made herself some eggs and toast and headed into the living room. While she ate, she put the TV on and started flicking channels.

After going through the entire roster of channels,

she settled on the entertainment network which had a post Emmys wrap up on. Sally half listened to what they said as she checked email on her phone. The mention of her boyfriend's name grabbed her attention, and she looked up from her cell.

"A newbie to the prime time red carpet was daytime super hunk Mark Martin accompanied by what could only be classified as a giant step down in the date department."

Sally stared in horror as a picture of her, looking like some poor cousin next to Dean, flashed on the screen. "The no-name woman definitely wasn't anything like the usual beauties he has as arm candy—"

Sally turned the TV off before she threw up. *So stupid.* She picked up the remote and hurled it across the room. Why did she agree to this in the first place? Over and over, she'd told Dean and Jodie she didn't fit, but, no, they said it would be fine. Well, they were wrong, and now she'd be a laughing stock. She couldn't do it anymore, pretend she and Dean fit together. It was an exercise in futility. He'd always be a stunning specimen of the human race, and she'd continue to age and look more frumpy as every year passed.

She got up and paced around the room. She didn't belong, never would. She'd been fooling herself to ever entertain the idea.

*My fantasy is over. Time to go home and be plain old Sally, school teacher.*

\*\*\*

Dean glanced at his girlfriend, sitting next to him. Ever since he'd returned from his interviews to pick her up, she'd been quiet. He'd asked her a couple times over lunch if she was all right, but she answered each time with "I'm tired." Still, he couldn't stop the niggling feeling it was something more.

He pulled into the parking lot for the airport. Once again, they were saying good-bye. He hated it, but, unfortunately, they both had jobs—his in LA and hers in Greenville, North Carolina.

He had plans in place—ones that meant being thousands of miles apart would become a thing of the past. He had a few commitments to fulfill first, though.

He hopped out of the car and walked around to Sally's side, opening her door for her. She didn't have any luggage other than her small carry-on, which she held in her hand. He grabbed her other hand in his and pulled her close. "Come on, sweetheart."

They walked in silence to the terminal, and, though her hand never left his, the fear she drifted farther away with every step wouldn't subside. He let her go while she checked in, but he made sure he could see her at all times.

When she returned, ticket in hand, she looked miserable. He pulled her into his arms and held her tight. She didn't soften into the hug, just stood stiff. He stepped back and studied her expression, almost one of grief.

He checked the departures board. She had a good hour before her flight was due to leave. "Why don't we go have a coffee and cake before you have to go?"

Although she didn't answer, she did let him take her hand and lead her to the Starbucks between two gift shops.

Once they each had coffee and a muffin, he found

a table at the back. "So, you going to tell me what is bugging you?"

She shook her head. "I just have a lot on my mind with school and everything."

"I know that's a lie. I'm not stupid." He wanted to shake some sense into her, make her tell him everything, but he was not that kind of man.

She huffed and threw her hands up in the air. "Fine. You want to know what's bothering me? It's you. You and your perfection and the perfection of everyone around you. Money, beauty. You have it all, and for us mere mortals, it's a lot to live up to."

Sally's words were harsh and unlike her. "Where is this coming from?"

"Last night was a lot, and I'm feeling very overwhelmed."

He could understand that. It had been a lot for him when he'd started in the industry. "It's not always like this. We are regular boring people most of the time."

She nodded, and he caught sight of the glistening in the corner of her eyes. *Fuck!*

He could handle a lot of things, but his woman in

tears wasn't one of them. He scooted his chair next to hers and wrapped his arms around her. She rested her head against his chest and cried.

He rubbed his hand up and down her back, powerless to do anything but be there for her. "It's going to be all right, sweetheart."

After a couple of minutes, her tears eased and she pulled away. "I'm sorry about your shirt."

He looked down to see a wet spot he hadn't even noticed. "I don't give a shit about that as long as you're all right."

"I will be." She wiped the last of tears away and blew her nose then looked at him and smiled. "I think it's time for me to go." He checked his watch, discovering she was right.

He held her close, tucked under his arm, as they walked to the security checkpoint. "I'm going to miss you, but I meant what I said. As soon as I can, I'll be winging my way to you."

She stood on tiptoe and kissed him. It wasn't sweet like usual. No, this time her kiss reeked of desperation. She pulled away and stared at him. "I don't think you should come to visit in a couple of weeks. I need some time to sort things out."

She moved away, not giving him a chance to plead his case. As she passed through security, a sense of dread hit him again. He needed to move Heaven and Earth to get to her as soon as possible because he might lose her for good if he didn't.

# Chapter Ten

Driving away from the airport, Dean's cell rang, and he clicked his Bluetooth to answer. "Hello?"

"Hey, it's Jerry. You finished at the airport yet?"

"Just leaving. Why?"

"I have some stuff I need you to look at. Can you come by my office?"

It wasn't like Jerry to ask him to come to his office, but he had nothing better to do, so he agreed. Twenty minutes later, he pulled into a roadside parking space in front of his office and made his way inside.

"So, what's so important it couldn't wait until our meeting next week?"

"Nothing really. Figured you'd go home and mope without your woman, so I'd be a good friend and distract you."

Dean hated his afternoon plans were so transparent. "I guess I should say thank you. Can I go now?"

"Nah. Since you're here, we can get started on the stuff that's been rolling in this morning."

"What stuff?"

"Scripts, my man. You're an Emmy winner now. You're hot property."

He could hardly believe one award win could change things so much, but when his manager dropped a pile of scripts on the table in front of him, reality hit. *That's way more than I receive in a normal year.* "This is great and all, but unless you can get me out of my *Love My Family* contract, I'm not even going to bother reading them."

"Done."

Dean stared at Jerry, not sure he'd heard him right. "What do you mean 'done'?"

"Just what I said. The moment you told me you didn't want to do it anymore, I started the negotiations to get you out of your contract. They have agreed as long as you are willing to film a few scenes to close out your story line."

"Really?"

His manager nodded. He couldn't stop himself from jumping up and doing a little happy dance. No more having to work regular hours in LA, which meant he could move to Greenville as soon as he could get things sorted out at this end. "You're brilliant. Do I ever tell you that?"

"Not often enough, considering I keep you employed."

"Well, I'm telling you right now. Best agent ever."

Dean needed to tell Sally and pulled out his phone to call her. Then his common sense kicked in. She would still be in the air. He would have to wait until she called him to tell him she'd arrived safely.

*\*\**

Sally managed to hold her shit together right up until she saw Jodie at the airport. Then the dam broke, and it all came pouring out. Jodie pulled her into a hug and held tight while the grief of what she'd decided overtook her.

"I'm not sure what all this is about, but do you think you can calm down enough for us to walk out to the car?"

Sally nodded then took a couple of deep breaths. Once she had her emotions under control, she followed Jodie to the car. All buckled in and ready to go, Jodie turned to her, a frown on her face. "Okay, missy, I'm not driving anywhere until you tell me what the waterworks are about."

She took a couple more steadying breaths of air. "I think Dean and I are through." The words were barely out of her mouth before the tears started again. Saying them aloud made them all the more real.

"What?"

"It was a nice fantasy while it lasted, but we don't work."

"Okay, you need to back it up a minute and start at the beginning because you're not making any sense."

She told her all the sordid details— everything the reporter said about her on TV, how ridiculous she looked standing next to him. How most of the people had ignored her at the ball like she was invisible.

They were too different to be together.

"And he broke up with you over that? Why—"

"No, no. I just can't be with him. It's too hard. I told him I need some time to sort things out."

Jodie crossed her arms over her chest and glared at Sally. "As your best friend, I say this with all of my love, but that is the biggest crock of shit I've ever heard."

"Excuse me?" A slap across her cheek from her best friend would have hurt less.

"You heard me. I didn't stutter."

"That's not what I meant, and you know it."

"Yes, I know. But seeing as you have decided to end a relationship with a man even blind person could tell loved you, I call bullshit."

"It's not bullshit we will never work." Sally's tears dried up, replaced with an all-encompassing fury.

"You're damn right, you won't, because you're too much of a scaredy cat."

"I am not!"

"Well then, get out your cell and call him and tell him you don't want to be with him anymore."

Sally stared at her hands in her lap. "I can't."

"Yes, you can. You're not incapable. I've seen you do it before."

"No, I mean I can't call him and tell him I don't want to be with him because it's not true."

"So, what's the problem if he wants you and you want him?"

"It's not so simple. Do you have any idea how much it hurt to hear those words about me on a national TV show? I just don't think I am built to withstand the battering of my self-esteem over a long period of time."

"Maybe you aren't, but you'll never know if you don't give it a go."

Jodie started the car and headed home. Sally needed time to wrap her head around everything. Maybe, in a few days, when it didn't hurt so much, she'd be able to deal with it.

\*\*\*

Dean stared at the time on his phone. Sally should have been home at least two hours ago and still she hadn't called him. He tapped the phone icon next to her name. The phone rang for a few seconds then clicked over to voice mail.

*Hi, this is Sally. I can't get to the phone right now, so please leave your name and number and I'll call you back as soon as I can.*

"Hey, sweetheart, I haven't heard from you. Just wanted to see if you made it home okay." He didn't know what else to say, so he hung up. The sense of dread that had crawled down his spine at the airport returned with a vengeance. Not once since he and Sally had met had he called and she hadn't picked up.

Three text messages and another phone call straight to voice mail later, Dean became officially worried. He rationalized she'd forgotten to turn her phone back on after the flight, but that didn't stop his worrying. He would have to wait until the morning and try again.

\*\*\*

Dean took a sip of coffee. He'd been up for half an hour, and it had taken every ounce of will power not to call Sally. She'd sent him a text message to let him know she'd made it home okay, but that was it. Somewhere in the middle of his restless night's sleep, he'd decided he would give her time to get in contact with him. His resolve was fading fast, though. He needed to hear her voice.

***

Dean dropped his keys on the table in the entryway. He'd been so distracted, filming hadn't been worth a damn and the reaming he'd gotten from the director well earned.

During his lunch break, he'd tried calling Sally again. A whole day and still nothing. He was going out of his mind.

He pulled his cell out of his pocket for the millionth time, still nada. One person could help him, and he scrolled through his contact list until he found her number then hit call.

The phone rang once before being answered. "I was wondering when I would hear from you."

Relief washed over Dean at the sound of Jodie's voice. "Hello to you, too. The fact you were even expecting my call scares the crap out of me."

"Listen, she's my best friend, and I'm only doing this because it's for her own good."

"You have to fill me in. What is going on? Sally is not answering any of my calls or returning any of my texts."

Jodie sighed. "Yeah, I know. I can't tell you everything because you need to sort this out between the two of you. But I will tell you this. You need to watch the entertainment network post Emmy wrap up."

"What on earth does that have to do with anything?"

"You're a smart guy. You'll figure it out."

Before he could ask anything else, the call disconnected.

# Chapter Eleven

**D**ean didn't waste a single second after speaking to Jodie. He ran to his office and pulled up the Internet. He googled the entertainment network, and, after a bit of searching, he found the episode Jodie had told him about.

He hated watching this crap. It was the bit he despised most about his job. After five minutes, he couldn't stomach listening, so he fast forwarded, hoping what he looked for would stand out.

A picture of him and Sally flashed on the screen, and he hit pause then rewound a little and hit play. With every second the pretty boy who thought he was all that listed the vicious unfounded things about Sally, Dean's rage built. How anyone could say such awful things, let alone about someone they didn't even know, was atrocious. He grabbed his cell and growled his manager's name.

"What's up?" Jerry asked, picking up after a couple of rings.

"I want the entertainment network blacklisted."

"Excuse me?"

"They ring you for an interview, a favor, anything, tell them to fuck off."

"Okay, man, but what's brought this on?"

"Did you see the entertainment network post Emmy wrap-up?"

"No, I haven't had a chance yet. Been busy dealing with scripts and calls from directors and casting agents. Why?"

He took a couple of deep breaths to calm down. This wasn't his manager's fault, and he shouldn't be yelling at him. "They said some awful things about Sally as my date for the Emmys, and now she is not talking to me. I love her, Jerry. I can't lose her."

"Cool, I get it. I'll make sure they get nothing from me when it concerns you. What else can I do?"

"Nothing really. I'll be out of town for the rest of

the week, so you may cop some grief from Brad."

"I'll handle it. Just go get your woman."

Dean said bye then hung up. He placed a quick call to Brad, explaining he had an emergency he needed to deal with but he'd back Monday and have his head on straight. That, of course, all hinged on Sally accepting his apology.

***

Sally cleaned the notes from her previous lesson off the board then started writing up the details of the assignment for the next class. The bell rang and the students of her AP English class strolled in. When the second bell rang, she turned to face the class and had to put her hand on her desk to stop from collapsing into a puddle on the floor. Just inside the door stood the one person she most definitely didn't want to see.

"What are you doing here?"

"You weren't answering my calls, and I was worried."

"You need to leave. I have a class to teach." She glanced at said students, and they stared, mouths agape. She'd already had to fend off a bunch of questions from students who'd seen her at the Emmys, and now every teenage girl's fantasy stood in their classroom.

Dean turned to her class. "I apologize for interrupting, but I need a moment of Ms. Austens' time if it's okay with you?"

A rousing chorus of yes echoed around the classroom. *Traitors. They are so getting a pop quiz.*

"And what if I don't want to talk to you."

"Please, Sally, let me explain." Dean had the most pathetic hangdog look on his face. It shouldn't make her want to hug and kiss him, but it did.

"Hear him out, Ms. Austens," Violet Stephens, one of those girls blessed with good looks and brains, called out. "You cannot turn away a man as fine as him."

All of the other students chuckled.

"Unless you want a pop quiz every day for the next week, you all need to stay out of this, and you"—she turned to face Dean—"need to wait in the hallway. I will be with you in a minute."

Dean stepped outside but stayed in the doorway

where he could be seen. She set her students to work then joined him, shutting the door behind her.

"You can't come barging into my class like this. I could lose my job."

"I'm sorry, but when you didn't return my calls, I needed to see you, and I couldn't wait another minute."

The miserable look on his face almost had her jumping into his arms and apologizing, but the reason she'd been ignoring his calls still existed. "I needed some space."

"I know. I saw the show. Furious doesn't even come close to explaining how I felt about what they said, and I am sorry you had to hear it. I wish you had told me."

She wanted to tell him it was fine and she'd never let something like this bother her again, but it would have been a lie. "It's hard. You're gorgeous. You couldn't possibly know how hurtful it is to have people judge you on the way you look."

"But I do know. You don't think people judge me on my appearance? Most think I'm some brainless muscle-bound idiot, but you and I both know the truth. Like I know you are the most amazing woman and a million times better than any of those plastic starlets I had escorted before."

Tears pooled in the corner of her eyes, but she wasn't going to let them fall. She'd cried enough in the last few days but not anymore. "That doesn't change the fact we live on different sides of the country. Every time I have to say good-bye, not knowing when I'll see you again, kills me."

"It kills me, too, and it's why I've quit my job." He took a step toward her. "As soon as I finish this movie I'm shooting, I'm moving to Greeneville."

She stared at him, not sure she'd heard him right. "Why would you do that?"

"Because I love you, Sally Austens. You are the one for me. When I look at my future twenty-five years from now, you are the one I see in my life."

*So much for not crying.* Tears ran down her cheeks. "Really?"

"Yes, really. I want you in my life, sweetheart, for now and forever." He dropped to his knee and pulled out a pale-blue box. "Sally, I love you, and it would make me the happiest man on earth if you would agree to be my wife."

*Oh fuck!*

Sally had hoped time and again for this exact moment. The man of her dreams on his knees, asking her to marry him. It was on the tip of her tongue to say no—it was too soon, and there was still too much to work out. But Jodie's words echoed in her head. *You're too much of a scaredy cat.*

*Not anymore.*

"Yes, yes. Dean, I will marry you. I love you, and I can think of nothing better than to spend the rest of my life with you."

He swept her up into a tight embrace and swung her around, setting her back on her feet after a full circle. A cheer sounded from inside her classroom. *Yep, definitely a pop quiz and an essay to go with it.*

"Thank you. Thank you so much." His lips collided with hers, and his hands around her waist were the only thing keeping her on her feet because her knees buckled with the pleasure.

She couldn't believe three months ago she'd been alone and facing life as a cat lady. Now, she had Dean and a wonderful future to look forward to. It had been a tough learning curve, and she was sure she had more to learn, but, with him by her side loving her, she could handle anything.

"So, what do we do now?"

He looked at her, a cheeky grin on his face. "Want to play hooky with me?"

# About the Author

Melissa Kendall is an almost forty year-old mother of two. She lives in Perth Western Australia the second most isolated capital city in the world with the nearest city over 2000km away. Predominantly a stay-at-home mum, she works a few hours a week as a software support consultant. She has always loved to read and write, and spent most of her teens writing poetry and short stories. Over the years, daily life got in the way and she lost the passion for it, but after the birth of her first child, Melissa discovered e-books and her interest in writing rekindled.

# Also by Melissa Kendall

Curve My Appetite

**The Castle Wolves**
No Such Thing as Can't
What She Needs
Not What He Thought

www.ingramcontent.com/pod-product-compliance
Lightning Source LLC
Chambersburg PA
CBHW060942120626
46557CB00003B/1101